CREEPERS

Pen Pals

by Edgar J. Hyde

Illustrations by Chloe Tyler

PAB-0608-0299 • ISBN: 978-1-4867-1875-7

Copyright ©2020 Flowerpot Press, a Division of Flowerpot Children's Press, Inc., Oakville, ON, Canada.

Printed and bound in the U.S.A.

Table of Contents

CHAPTER ONE

The Note

"Natasha Morris, will you please tell me, and the rest of your classmates, what on earth is so interesting outside?"

With a jolt, Natasha turned toward the teacher.

"I'm sorry, Miss Harrison, I was just thinking about..." Natasha's voice trailed off.

She couldn't think of an excuse, and she couldn't possibly tell the truth—that this morning's long-winded history lesson was boring! After all, wasn't history supposed to be about Henry VIII and his six wives, romance, divorce, and gory beheadings? Instead she was having to sit and listen for two hours about crop rotation! Crop rotation—who cares?

"No. Don't even bother stuttering your way through an excuse, just do me a favor and pay attention. Remember you have a test coming up next week, and crop rotation just might be one of the questions!" Miss Harrison turned to the rest of the class. "Now, where were we?" Her voice droned on and on.

Olivia turned and smiled at Natasha sympathetically. The two were best friends and had been since they first met up as four-year-olds in the same preschool. They were now in their first year of high school, enjoying feeling grown-up, carrying their books from class to class around the massive, never-ending hallways, giggling as they frequently got lost, only to arrive red and breathless to their next class. They had made new friends, too.

There was Ellis, with her dark curly hair and large brown eyes. Natasha envied her. Then there was Marcie, though Natasha couldn't make up her mind about her just yet. She was the complete opposite of Ellis, pale with long, straw-like blonde hair and somewhat on the quiet side. Pale and interesting, I guess, if you were being nice, thought Natasha.

She hastily scribbled a note and passed it to Olivia without Miss Harrison noticing.

Meet you outside the library at four.

Olivia quickly pushed the note inside her notebook and gave no sign of having received anything.

Natasha looked at her watch. Ten minutes past four. Where on earth was Olivia? Just then, she saw Olivia, Marcie, and Ellis wind their way up the long path from the front of the school.

"You took your time." She smiled as all three girls stopped just beside her.

"Sorry, Natasha, it's my fault," said Ellis. "I left my new favorite lip gloss in the bathroom and had to go get it. You never know who you might see on the way home."

Ellis was always experimenting with lip gloss and eye shadow and always on the lookout for free samples. She would come to school drenched in perfume, having spent the weekend in the perfume department of the nearest store.

"You should try some, Marcie. Look, it's a pale pink, it'd look great on you."

"Gosh, no," said Marcie. "My mom would freak out. She says there's plenty of time to put all that 'junk,' as she calls it, on my face. Anyway, I'd rather keep my money for important things. I'm going to buy some new headphones this weekend, at least they will last longer than your makeup will!"

"Hey, Ellis," someone shouted from behind them. The girls turned to see Scott Gregson across from them. He was the best looking guy in their grade, and everyone had their eye on him. "If you're going home, I'll walk with you."

Ellis smiled. "See what the 'junk' on your face does for you, girls," she muttered. "Sure, Scott, I was just saying goodbye to the girls. See you tomorrow, everybody." And off she went, pink lips glistening, dark curls bouncing, backpack slung casually over her arm.

"Don't you just wish you had her confidence," sighed Olivia.

"Yes, and her hair and her teeth and her eyes," replied Natasha. "Never mind, 'Make the best of what you've got' is what my mom always says. Now let's see, what could you make out of the three of us?"

And as the three started to make their way home, they laughed together, picking out the parts of each other that they thought were the "best."

"Okay, Natasha," said Olivia, "you give me your tiny waist, Marcie can give me her small perfectly shaped feet, and I can probably get away with using my own hands—if I paint my fingernails—and with the help of a wig, there we have it, the perfect girl!"

And so the conversation carried on until the girls were almost home.

"Oh, and Natasha," Olivia began, "next time you write me a note in class, you really don't have to write my full name on it. I know who I am!"

Natasha looked at Olivia. "I didn't write your full name, Olivia. In fact, I didn't even write your first name!"

"Yes, you did," Olivia laughed, as she fished in both jacket pockets for the note. "You wrote, 'Olivia Goulden, meet you outside the library at four.' Darn, I can't find the note—oh, look, here it is."

They had now reached Marcie's house and Olivia had emptied the contents of her backpack onto the pavement outside. She showed the hastily scrawled note to Natasha and sure enough, Olivia's name was written above what Natasha remembered writing.

Olivia Goulden,
Meet you outside the library at four.

"That's really weird, Olivia. I don't remember writing that, it doesn't even look like my handwriting."

"Marcie, where have you been?" the girls heard Marcie's mom shout from an upstairs window.

"Oops, gotta go! Mom wants me to go to the grocery store with her today. See you tomorrow."

"Bye, Marcie," called the two girls as she disappeared inside her front door.

Natasha was still staring at the note.

"Stop trying to be funny, Natasha. I mean if you passed the note straight to me and I didn't add my own name to it, then who did?" Olivia protested. "Anyway, look, I have to run too. I'm babysitting Mrs. Winter's twins tonight, and I have to try and get my homework done before I go. I'll see you tomorrow."

"All right," sighed Natasha, "but I still don't understand."

She left Olivia at the end of the street where the road leading to her house forked left.

Weird, she thought as she walked, she must have been in more of a bored stupor than she realized this morning. How could you write someone's name and not remember?

"Suzanna Craigson," she read aloud from one of the gravestones in the cemetery. She had to pass the cemetery every morning and afternoon going to and from school, and although she was never comfortable with it, she found the best way around it was to make up stories about the people lying beneath the rows and rows of tombstones. That way it took the scariness out of it.

"Born November 2, 1806. Cruelly taken from her beloved parents November 1, 1820."

Natasha had never noticed that particular stone before, or maybe it was just that she had never

actually realized how young Suzanna had been when she died.

Wonder what happened to her, she thought. The use of the word "cruelly" seemed to indicate murder or something gory and horrible.

Better stop thinking about it, she decided. Mom always says my imagination's too vivid. It'll end up getting me into trouble one of these days.

✍   ✍   ✍

"Here comes fatso, here comes fatso." Her young brother's chanting soon stopped her daydreaming.

"Come here, Tommy, you little brat," she laughed, chasing the bubbly little three-year-old into the backyard. "I'll show you fatso."

She grabbed him and hugged him tightly around the waist, lifting him right off his feet. She kissed him loudly on the lips and came away covered in green sticky goo.

"What have you been eating now?" She smiled.

"Gooey monsters," he said and showed her the

empty packet in his tiny hand.

"Green Slimy Guts," she read aloud. "Made from jelly and packets of sugar and full of additives." She added, "Your teeth will fall out," and poked him in the tummy playfully.

"Don't care about teef," he retorted. "Like gooey monsters!"

How did the rhyme go, she mused as she went inside to change. Sugar and spice and all things nice, oh yes, frogs and snails and puppy dogs' tails, or something like that. Tommy was that, all right, and she adored every last little inch of him. She wondered if Suzanna Craigson had had a brother.

CHAPTER TWO

Look Out!

The next morning, Natasha simply couldn't believe they were having to play soccer outside in the rain. It had started to rain last night and hadn't let up from then until now, so the field was virtually flooded! Their gym teacher, however, had insisted that they change and "get on out there! Rain never hurt anyone!" So there they were, trying desperately to run around, but usually ending up sprawled on the ground with the ball and legs flying every way but the right way!

Natasha walked over to where Olivia was standing near the goal. Both Olivia and Marcie hated sports of any kind and were both trying to look small and insignificant so that Miss Starrs wouldn't notice they weren't participating in the game.

"Managing to get away with it so far?" she hissed at the pair.

Olivia raised her eyes up. "I'm so wet and dirty, I'll have to soak in a hot bubble bath for at least three hours tonight!"

Natasha laughed. Just then, one of the girls at the far end of the field started to run toward them. As she drew nearer, Natasha realized that the girl was Ellis, wearing a brand new bright orange and green headband. Ellis drew her foot back and kicked the ball as hard as she could.

The ball seemed to be heading straight for Olivia. Natasha moved forward to try and stop it, but to her surprise, Marcie moved out in front of her. She took a swipe at the ball, but misjudging the wet ground, leaned too far forward, causing herself to skid in the mud. She slid far down the field, turning around to face the opposite direction. The ball flew through the air. Natasha grabbed Olivia.

"Olivia, look out!" she shouted as both girls fell to the ground waiting for the sickening thud.

The ball landed just beside Natasha's right foot, narrowly missing hitting either of the girls, on almost the exact spot where Olivia had been standing a few short seconds before.

Miss Starrs was running down the field, wet hair standing straight up, eyes wide with horror, unsure whether or not anyone had been hurt.

"Natasha, Olivia, are you all right? Oh, thank goodness!" she said as both girls stood up. Both their faces were streaked with mud, their gym shorts and T-shirts dirty and soaked. "Go inside and take a hot shower, girls," she said gently, "while I attend to Marcie."

Marcie too was on her feet. "I'm sorry, Olivia, Miss Starrs, I was only trying to block..." She was crying now, her pale cheeks even paler than normal.

"Go inside, Marcie," said Miss Starrs. "Go ahead, follow the girls in and take a hot shower. I'll come and see you all in a minute or two."

Miss Starrs gently herded the girls into the school then went back to the top of the field. She checked her watch—only about ten minutes to go. She'd let the three girls have some time to themselves and then get the rest of the class inside and cleaned up. She blew the whistle for the girls to play on and heaved a sigh of relief. She'd thought her recently completed first aid course was finally going to come in handy! She looked around to see where Ellis went; Miss Starrs knew she hadn't meant any harm, but since she was the one who kicked the offending ball, she was sure she'd be concerned about Olivia.

She finally spotted her, standing on her own on one side of the field. Now isn't that strange. Miss Starrs shook her head. She had thought Olivia and Ellis were friends. Maybe she was wrong. She tried to shake some of the rain from her hair and ran up the field to make sure nothing else was going on.

Ellis admired her new tennis shoes. She thought the green flash on the side matched her new headband really well.

🌧   🌧   🌧

Marcie was drying off after her warm shower. The girl was shaking from the shock of what had almost happened.

"I really am sorry, Olivia," she kept repeating. "I was only trying to block the shot. I could see from where I was standing that Ellis was going to make a direct hit. I mean, I don't mean that she meant to hit you, just that I could see that it looked like...Oh, I don't know what I mean anymore. I really am so sorry," she finished.

Olivia put her arms around the tearful girl.

"Look, Marcie, I really appreciate what you did out there just now. But the truth is that no harm was done and I'm eternally grateful to you for getting me off that cold, wet field and into this warm shower, so no more tears, okay?"

Marcie smiled. "Okay, if you're sure you forgive me."

"And, hey," joked Natasha, "aren't you a dark horse? I thought you hated soccer, yet there you were, diving in front of people, going after balls— quite the little athletic heroine. Just shows what friends will do for you. You're lucky, Olivia," she finished.

Marcie looked apprehensive but when she realized that Natasha was genuinely congratulating her, she visibly relaxed.

"Let's get dressed and get out of here," said Olivia, "before the rest of the class comes in and we're caught up in the stampede. And remember we have to pick up our class photos today. I can't wait to see how awful we look and who has the worst acne!"

CHAPTER THREE

Class Photo

Marcie volunteered to pick up all three photos and got in line outside the principal's office. Ellis was two people in front of her.

"Hey, Marcie, how are you doing now?" She smiled. "That was some display you put on this morning."

"I'm okay," Marcie replied. "You must have been a little shaken up when you realized the direction the ball was going."

"Next," came the loud voice from just inside the principal's office before Ellis could reply.

Ellis stepped forward.

"See you later, Marcie," she said as she picked up

her photo and walked off down the hallway.

Marcie sighed. Why was she feeling so guilty about this whole incident when Ellis had played an obvious part and yet seemed to be shrugging the whole thing off? Maybe that was what happened when boys became interested in you—soccer fields became an insignificant part of your life and lip gloss took over. She wondered if she'd ever feel that way, but couldn't help but question whether boys would ever be interested in her. Maybe she should dye her hair.

👄   👄   👄

Marcie handed the small package to Natasha.

"I gave Olivia hers." Marcie was out of breath from hurrying down the hallway. "She says she'll see you in class. I've got geography, so I'll catch up with you later."

"Thanks, Marcie, see you later." Natasha stuffed the photo in her backpack—she'd have more time to look at it later.

She took her place in Mr. Jenkins' French class, as usual sitting somewhere near Olivia.

She liked French, and even more so since Mr. Jenkins was more than a little good-looking. She could listen to his almost perfect accent and look at his ruggedly handsome face every day and not fall asleep once! She smiled briefly at Olivia before opening her textbook.

Just before the end of the school day, Natasha realized she'd forgotten to pick up the dry cleaning her mom had asked her to pick up when she was half asleep that morning. She'd have to run all the way if she was going to make it before it closed. She hoped Olivia remembered they had plans for this evening. She'd pass her a note, just in case. The bell rang and Natasha jumped up right away. She pressed the note into Olivia's hand.

"Got to run," she said. "See you later."

Olivia clasped the note as she tried not to drop

her books, pens, and backpack and watched Natasha almost run from the classroom.

I wonder where she is going in such a rush, Olivia thought. I'll find out tonight, I guess.

"Did you pick up the dry cleaning?" Natasha's mom shouted, as the front door slammed.

"Yes, Mom, I remembered," Natasha shouted back, breathing a sigh of relief that her memory hadn't failed her!

She gave Tommy's sleeping face a quick kiss as she passed his room. He really wore himself out so he still needed a short afternoon nap. Then she went into her own room to change out of her dreaded uniform. Sweatpants and T-shirt on, she flopped onto her bed, hands behind her head.

I guess I better check if I have any homework now because I probably won't get around to doing it later, she thought, picking up her backpack. As she rummaged around in the bag, she found the forgotten class photo.

Oh, the class photo, she smiled. This should be hilarious, if previous years are anything to go by, she thought.

She tore off the cellophane and searched the sea of faces for her own. There she was, hair pushed behind her ears with little wisps escaping from either side. She could never get it to look even remotely smooth, except for the year her mom had taken her to the salon to have it put up for a school dance she was going to. The girl at the salon had tried her best, but even she had a hard time getting it under control. There had been so much hairspray on it that Natasha decided she preferred it to look messy rather than stuck together on top of her head!

But look, there was Ellis and Olivia standing together and Marcie in the front row. She was smaller than the others, so the photographer had suggested it would be better for her to be toward the front of the class. Marcie said later she should have worn her new platform shoes, then she wouldn't have had to be split up from her friends. Ellis had smiled at this, though not as widely as she had smiled for the cameraman. She was so photogenic; just look at the way she looked at the camera.

Natasha's eyes scanned the rest of the photograph quickly. Her eyes came to rest on the right-hand side of the back row. A small, pale girl stood slightly apart from the others, her eyes not looking into the camera at all.

Who on earth is that? thought Natasha. She'd never seen the girl before. Was it someone from another grade who'd been put with theirs at the last minute? She didn't remember anyone being brought in. Or maybe it was someone new altogether, but no, new students always caused such a stir, she couldn't possibly have missed out on that happening. Who was she? Olivia would surely know.

She looked at her watch—only five-thirty. Olivia was supposed to come over at about seven that night. They were going to plan their costumes for the Halloween dance on Friday night. Natasha wanted to go as Cleopatra, the Queen of the Nile, and her mom had promised to help make her wig. It would also be a good excuse to put lots of makeup on and wear jewelry halfway up her arms!

She put the photo back in her backpack and went downstairs to find a snack.

CHAPTER FOUR

Another Note

Olivia looked again at the note.

See you at seven at the cemetery— look for Suzanna Craigson's tombstone.

Olivia was utterly confused by the note. She thought tonight was for discussing costumes, not an eerie night at the cemetery! It was so unlike Natasha, too. She wasn't exactly brave when it came to anything to do with graves and old cemeteries, and especially not at seven o'clock at night, just when it was beginning to get dark.

Olivia sighed a deep sigh and stuffed the note

into her jacket pocket. After she helped her mom clear the dishes, she'd get changed and go meet her friend, no doubt all would be revealed once she met up with Natasha.

Five minutes past seven. Natasha was late. Olivia had found the tombstone fairly easily as it was positioned near the front of the graveyard and could be seen clearly from the road. Olivia was grateful she'd worn her heavy jacket because it was beginning to get really cold. She pulled up her collar and dug her hands deeper into her pockets.

At ten past seven, Olivia heard a voice.

"Olivia." She turned and saw a figure come from the direction of the cemetery gate.

"Hurry up, Natasha," she said. "What were you doing in there?"

It was in that split second, she told Natasha later, that she realized "Natasha" wasn't in fact Natasha at all. The person coming toward her was smaller than her friend, and she walked with a pronounced limp. Olivia tried to see the girl more clearly, but dusk had just started to fall and she couldn't quite make out her features.

As she approached, slowly, hindered by the limp, Olivia was able to see that the girl had long, almost golden, hair, curled in ringlets that framed her face and cascaded down her back, and she appeared to be in trouble.

"Are you okay?" Olivia asked.

The last thing she felt like doing was standing there offering to help; for some reason, the approaching girl frightened her. Olivia shivered.

Don't be such a baby, she thought. It's just the fact that you're right beside a cemetery, it's getting dark, and the trees are casting dark shadows.

This little conversation with herself only made her feel worse though, and she found herself hoping Natasha would hurry up. A bit of moral support would be great!

The girl had stopped now, almost directly across from Olivia, and Olivia was aware of the strange clothes the girl was wearing. Her dress was long and frilled at the cuffs and she wore a little matching bonnet over her curls. She wore a funny built up shoe on her right foot, and this was the leg which had seemed to drag behind her as she walked.

The girl looked directly at Olivia and Olivia noticed for the first time there was an almost ethereal quality about her. Her skin was so pale that it was almost translucent and her eyes seemed to be wet with tears.

"Are you Olivia Goulden?" she almost whispered. "I must find her, please help me. She is in great danger, I must warn her!"

She reached out her hand toward Olivia's but it didn't touch her. Instead, the girl's hand seemed to go right through Olivia's, bringing with it a cold sensation and cold wind which chilled her very soul.

Olivia was by now literally frozen to the spot

with fear. She was so cold that her teeth began to chatter and all she could think was she had to get out of there.

"Please, you must listen to me," the girl said again. It was at this point that Olivia was unfrozen. She turned from the pale haired girl and ran faster than she had ever run before. All the way along the pavement she ran, sometimes stumbling over cracks, until at last she could see Natasha's house, warm and welcoming in the distance.

She didn't even knock on the door, she just burst in and ran straight upstairs to Natasha's bedroom, pushing Natasha aside as she jumped up to see what the commotion was.

"Olivia, what on earth...?"

Olivia was standing next to the window and had pulled back the curtain.

"Turn off the light," she instructed Natasha.

"Not until you tell me what's happening," Natasha replied from the bed where she had fallen.

"Turn off the light!" Olivia almost screamed. "Or I'll do it myself!"

"All right, all right," answered Natasha as she jumped up to flip the switch. "Keep your voice down, you'll wake Tommy." She joined Olivia at the bedroom window to look outside, although she had no idea what she was looking for.

"Look, there she is!" Olivia was almost hysterical.

Natasha looked out of the window to see Marcie approaching the house.

"It's Marcie," said Natasha. "She called just after six o'clock tonight to ask if she could come over and help with our costumes. What's wrong with that?"

It was then that she noticed that Olivia's hands, and practically her whole body, were shaking.

"Olivia, you have to calm down and tell me what happened out there—I have no idea what's going on. Come on, come and sit on the bed with me."

Olivia allowed herself to be led to the bed where she promptly sat down and burst into tears.

Marcie had arrived and knocked on the front door. Tommy woke up and started to cry. Mrs. Morris answered the door and brought Marcie in.

"Do me a favor, sweetie," she said, "go and start heating some milk for Tommy. He likes a hot milky drink if he wakes up at this time. I'll go and get him."

"Sure, Mrs. Morris," agreed Marcie. She just adored chubby little Tommy and didn't mind helping out with him before she joined her friends upstairs.

Olivia, meanwhile, had just recounted her story to her friend.

"But what on earth were you doing standing in the cemetery?" asked Natasha.

Olivia turned, aghast, to Natasha. "Because you told me to meet you there, in your note," she replied.

"In my note. What note? The one I passed you in French?"

Oh no, not again, thought Natasha. Was she going crazy? "Let me see the note, Olivia. I know I didn't ask to meet you at the cemetery, I just know I didn't. Let me see the note, please."

Olivia took the now tattered note from her jacket pocket and handed it to her friend. Sure enough, the note said what Olivia had said it did, except that, for Natasha, it was even more frightening.

See you at seven at the cemetery —— look for Suzanna Craigson's tombstone.

Suzanna Craigson! The grave Natasha had noticed for the first time the other day. Natasha shook her head in disbelief.

"I have no idea what on earth is going on here, Olivia, I swear. I did not write 'at the cemetery' on that note, I just wrote 'See you at seven.' I mean, you know how I feel about graves and things, there's just no way I would have asked you to hang around there waiting for me." She sighed deeply. "I don't know what to do, Olivia, you do believe me don't you?"

Natasha looked at her friend.

Olivia lifted tear-stained eyes. "Yes, Natasha, but only because it's you and I've known you too long to think you would ever deliberately frighten me. But it still doesn't solve the mystery. What on earth is happening here? First, my full name was written on the initial note, then words are seemingly added to the second note and then that person outside just now..." Olivia started to shake again.

"We'd better get ourselves together before Marcie joins us—we don't want to frighten her to death with some half-baked story about notes and ghostly apparitions," said Natasha.

"Half-baked story?" protested Olivia.

"Yes, I know what you saw, and I believe you," said Natasha, "but will anybody else? Honestly, we should keep this whole thing under wraps until we know exactly what's going on."

"So what's Ellis coming to the party as?" asked

Marcie as she glued some more sequins on Olivia's dress. Olivia had decided to go as a gangster girl. She was a real old movie buff and had just finished watching a slew of gangster movies where all the girls wore sequined dresses, fur stoles, and glossy red lipstick.

"Don't know—she hasn't mentioned it at all," replied Olivia.

"Don't think for a minute it'll be anything less than glamorous though. I can't imagine Ellis doing anything remotely unglamorous, can you?"

Natasha smiled. "Well, we're not exactly dressing down for the event, are we?" She looked at Marcie. "What are you coming as, Marcie? Hey, listen, if you don't have a costume yet, why don't you come as Al Capone? You know, the infamous Chicago gangster, then you could match Olivia. You could borrow some of my dad's stuff. Marcie, are you listening to a word I'm saying?"

"Yes, Natasha, I hear you," she replied. "And

thanks. It's just that my mom said she would find a costume for me—something about family tradition." Marcie lowered her head again and returned to the task at hand.

Natasha and Olivia exchanged glances but said nothing. Sometimes they wondered about Marcie's family. She seemed to have a very strict upbringing—maybe because she was an only child they guessed.

Olivia threw a rolled up leather belt in Natasha's direction. "Made you this, Natasha. It's an asp. Remember, Cleopatra needs a snake."

Natasha screamed loudly. "Get that away from me, Olivia! There's no way I'm putting an asp near me—Cleopatra or not!"

Natasha's bedroom door was pushed open to reveal Mrs. Morris standing in the hallway.

"If you girls wake Tommy again you won't be going to the Halloween dance," she threatened. "Now keep it down, please."

CHAPTER FIVE

Library Research

The next day at school, Natasha, Olivia, and Ellis stood chatting in the hallway.

"Still going out with Scott, Ellis?" Olivia asked.

"Yes, we went to the movies last night and saw a really scary movie, you know the one about the zombies in the mall?"

"Zombies? Are you nuts?" laughed Natasha. "I thought couples were supposed to go see romantic movies and sit in the back row?"

Ellis laughed. "I know, I don't actually think Scott and I are going to work out. I'd rather sit and watch a good scary movie than make out in the back row. Olivia, is something wrong?"

Olivia had turned from the two girls and was staring at Marcie who was walking slowly toward them. Except that she wasn't walking, she was limping and dragging her leg behind her.

"Wh-what did you do to your leg?" Olivia stammered.

Marcie made her way to the girls.

"I fell down getting out of the shower last night. The floor was wet and I slid," she finished. "I have to go," she said. "I've got social studies first period and you know what Mr. Livingstone's like."

"Bye, Marcie," the girls shouted as they watched her disappear up the stairs and down the hall.

"I have to run, too," said Ellis. "See you at lunch."

"Bye, Ellis," said Natasha. "Olivia, are you all right?" she asked her friend.

Olivia shivered. "Yes, I'm okay, Natasha. It's just that with the color of Marcie's hair, and then the limp, she looked just like…"

"It's okay, Olivia, I know who you mean. Suzanna

Craigson's on my mind too, but I'm trying hard not to think about her."

Just then, the bell rang summoning the girls to class.

"Let's go." Natasha took her friend's arm. "We can talk more about this later."

📢   📢   📢

Natasha spent the whole first two periods decorating her notebook with drawings of eyes. Cleopatra's eyes with thick black liner and gold lashes, Cleopatra's eyes with thick green liner and blue lashes, Cleopatra's eyes with thick silver liner and gold lashes! She was just debating whether or not to paint her nails two different colors when she was startled by the bell ringing. She stuffed her books into her backpack and as she did, she came across the class photo she had put into her bag the previous evening so that she could ask Olivia who the mystery girl was.

Natasha met up with Olivia in the lunch line.

"Wait until I show you this!" Natasha took the class photo from inside her bag and showed it to Olivia.

"Notice anything strange?" she asked her friend.

Olivia scanned the photograph.

"Oh my God, it's her!" she stammered. "Natasha, that's her, the girl from the graveyard, the one at the top of the photo." She turned to Natasha. "I don't understand—what's going on here?"

People were turning around to stare.

"Shh, Olivia." Natasha again took her friend's arm and guided her away from the line toward the hall.

"What on earth do you mean? I can't believe what I'm hearing," said Natasha. "Do you mean the girl in the photo is Suzanna Craigson?"

Olivia was no longer listening; instead, she was rummaging through her own backpack.

"Here it is," she said triumphantly, as she pulled out her own copy of the class picture. She pulled the cellophane from the print and thrust it in front of Natasha's eyes.

"Look," she cried. "She's not in my photo. There's nothing weird about mine. Who's been tampering with yours? None of this is making any sense. Who would want to paint a face on your photo? Who is this Suzanna Craigson?" She started to cry.

Natasha took Olivia's photo and looked at it long and hard. Sure enough, the girls in the back row of this photo were all classmates and there was no sign of the girl who stood at the top right-hand corner.

"I don't know the answers to any of your questions, Olivia, but I want to find out just as much as you do. Whoever Suzanna Craigson is, we're going to find out, and find out soon. Come on, don't cry anymore, it's all right."

Olivia wiped her eyes with the sleeve of her jacket. Natasha held both the photos in her hands. She must stay calm, for Olivia's sake, as well as her own. She turned the photographs over and saw that

Olivia's name was written on Natasha's copy and vice versa. Marcie must have mixed up the prints when she picked them up the previous day.

"Olivia, it looks like you had my copy," she said. "Look, your name's on mine." She showed the backs of both photos to the girl. "Not that it matters," she finished.

"Oh, but it does," Olivia replied. "Don't you see? Suzanna said she had to talk to me, that I was in great danger. She seems to be trying to contact me somehow, adding things to your notes, appearing outside the cemetery, and now appearing in my picture! I don't know if I can take much more of this." Olivia was white as a ghost.

Natasha tried to appear reassuring. "Come on," she said purposefully, "we have two more classes then you and I, my friend, are going to the library."

"We're meeting Ellis, and probably Marcie, though Natasha."

"Darn," said Natasha. "Well, we'll just have to

wait then. No more notes." She smiled. "We'll make our plans face-to-face from now on!"

"Why are we going there anyway?" asked Olivia.

"Because they keep old newspapers, things of interest that happened in town in the past, and if there's anything about Suzanna Craigson, we're going to find it."

Olivia shuddered. Thank goodness Natasha was so brave and sensible, or at least pretending to be, because Olivia wasn't coping with this thing very well at all. Natasha replaced the two photos inside her backpack as both girls made their way to their next class. Neither she nor Olivia noticed that the girl at the top right corner of Olivia's class photograph had completely faded out of sight.

Mrs. Florence looked at both girls over the rim of her glasses. "Don't usually see you two young ladies in the library after school," she stated.

Natasha sighed. "I know, Mrs. Florence, but we've

decided to take part in a new project—life back in the 1800s right here in our own little town, and we thought you'd be the best person to help us out. Not that I'm insinuating that you're old or anything," she continued, "just that maybe you could point us in the direction of any old newspapers, history books, old pictures, et cetera, that could help us out."

The seemingly cold, but kind-hearted librarian almost smiled.

"This way then, girls." She led them toward the narrow winding staircase of the old library. "Hurry, before any other potential knowledge seekers come in looking for assistance."

The girls had never been upstairs in the library before. Indeed, it wasn't one of their most favorite places at all. They could always find much more exciting things to do outside of school, or at least up until now!

"When you reach the top, the books on your left will help with the history of the actual town, then the shelves below have hanging files which should contain old newspapers in chronological order, which I don't want messed up!" she added before returning to the main desk. "If you need any help, you'll have to come down. I really can't leave the desk unmanned in case it gets busy."

Her words faded into the distance as the two girls climbed higher and higher up into the upper level of the old library.

Natasha and Olivia exchanged glances.

"Busy?" Natasha raised her eyebrows. "When was the last time you saw a line form outside the library?"

Olivia giggled. "Shh, she'll hear you, and we may need her help later, you never know."

"She won't hear us," replied Natasha. "Listen, can't you hear her, 'stamp, stamp.' She just loves putting that 'overdue' stamp on the returned books."

The girls had by now reached their destination.

"Gosh, what a musty smell," said Olivia as she

plonked herself down on the dusty floor.

"It'll get even worse by the time we're finished," returned Natasha. "Just look at how thick the dust is on top of this book."

She pulled a large brown book from one of the top shelves and opened it on the desk in front of her.

"Okay, Olivia, you start with the newspapers. Now let's see, if I remember correctly, Suzanna lived from November 1806 to November 1820, so see if you can find anything about her from the papers. Here." She drew two bags of chips from inside her jacket pocket. "Sustenance."

Two hours later, the girls had made little progress. The name Craigson, Natasha had discovered, was relatively new to the town. The family had settled there in a house with a description that meant nothing to either of the girls. They decided that the house must no longer exist or, if it did, it had been changed so much by the present owner that it bore

no resemblance to the description in the book.

"Wait a minute!" said Olivia excitedly. "Look at this!"

> TRAGEDY WITHIN CRAIGSON HOUSEHOLD.
>
> A YOUNG GIRL WAS TODAY RECOVERED FROM THE BOATING POND OUTSIDE HER HOME AT GATEFELLS AFTER A FATAL DROWNING INCIDENT.

Natasha slammed her book shut and gave her full attention to what Olivia was reading.

"That's where Ellis lives, Gatefells. Go on, Olivia, don't stop there."

> MR. AND MRS. CRAIGSON, WHO TODAY LOST THEIR ONLY CHILD, ARE UNDERSTANDABLY DISTRAUGHT AND HAVE ASKED THAT THEY BE LEFT ALONE WITH THEIR GRIEF.

The story stopped there, though in a later article the girls were able to read more about the family.

Apparently not much was known of the couple,

being relative newcomers to town, although Mr. Craigson was fast becoming a well-known figure in the community through his tireless work helping charitable organizations. They found that the girl who had drowned had, indeed, been named Suzanna. She had gone out on her own in the boat, despite having been warned by her parents on previous occasions that she should always be accompanied. If she had been accompanied by someone, there was no evidence of this. The article also said that she was in poor health and wore a built up shoe as she had been born with one leg shorter than the other.

Olivia inhaled sharply. "It's got to be the same person, Natasha, the girl in the photograph and at the gravesite. But why is she trying to reach me now? Oh, I wish I understood what was going on. It wasn't so long ago that I didn't even believe in ghosts!"

Natasha continued to flick through several newspapers. "At least we've found out some information, Olivia. The day hasn't been a total waste. I mean, we now know that Suzanna Craigson did live here and that she was killed in a boating accident and that she was very young." She stopped.

"So what, Natasha? I mean, I'm sorry, but how exactly does that help us figure out why on earth she wants to get in touch with me?" Olivia sighed.

"Relax, we'll get to the bottom of this little mystery soon enough," Natasha replied. "And, hey, did you notice those dates? November 2, 1806 to November 1, 1820—that means she died the day before her birthday, the day after Halloween. That has to have some significance. It's too creepy not to. Come on, let's get out of here before we get put back up on the shelves with the rest of the old relics in here! I feel so dusty, I can't wait to get home and take a shower."

The two girls climbed back down the winding staircase, dusting themselves off as they went.

"Thanks, Mrs. Florence," they shouted to the

librarian as they headed for the door.

"Shh, girls." She held her finger to her lips.

"Sorry," they giggled, "didn't think there was anyone here to disturb." As indeed there wasn't.

Luckily for them, Mrs. Florence didn't hear their last remark.

She followed them to the door. "I hope you put everything back in chronological order." She bent over to talk to the two girls. "I put in a lot of hard work organizing those papers, you know," she finished.

"Yes, of course we did." Natasha smiled. "Thank you for all your help, Mrs. Florence. We might need to come back another day, and it's great to know you'll be here for us to rely on," she gushed.

Mrs. Florence pushed a loose tendril of hair back behind her glasses. "Always a pleasure to see you both," she flushed. "Come back whenever you like, girls." She closed the door gently behind them both.

"Natasha?" said Olivia as they crossed the road

outside the library to begin the journey home.

"Yes?" said Natasha absentmindedly.

"What does chronological mean?"

CHAPTER SIX

Let's Dance

Olivia was excited about the Halloween dance tonight and felt as though her geography lesson would never end. She and Natasha both had their costumes ready and couldn't wait to get home and dress up.

"I wonder what Marcie and Ellis are doing. Maybe they told Natasha and she forgot to say, or maybe it's a big secret," Olivia mused.

Both she and Natasha had made a pact to forget all about Suzanna Craigson for this one night and simply go to the Halloween dance and have fun!

The bell began to ring and the students threw books, pens, and anything else they had in their bags.

Olivia caught up with Natasha outside the class. "Thought that was never going to end!" She smiled at her friend.

Natasha smiled back. "Hey, Ellis," she called.

Olivia looked in the direction Natasha was facing and saw Ellis' retreating back as she left the school building. Her dark curls bobbed as she flounced out of the door but she didn't seem to hear her friends as she kept walking.

"Strange," said Natasha. "I could have sworn she saw us, and I'm almost positive she's not far enough away that she wouldn't have heard me yell." She looked confused for a second or two. "Oh well, let's get out of here. We have a lot to do before we meet up tonight, and then we'll discover the secrets behind Marcie's and Ellis's costumes!"

The gymnasium was brightly lit, not just by lights but by strategically placed pumpkins with the insides removed to make room for short, dim candles. One by one, the students arrived, gushing over each others' costumes and guessing the identity of those who wore masks. Loud music filled the gym from the speakers set up on the stage and banners suspended from the ceiling had the words "Welcome to the Annual Halloween Dance" written on them.

Natasha was just arriving and was trying to adjust her wig as she got out of her mother's car.

"For Heaven's sake, Natasha, leave it alone or you'll end up with no wig on at all!" her mother sighed.

"Bye, Cleo." Tommy smiled from the backseat, his little fingers opening and closing over his chubby little hand as he waved goodbye. He couldn't quite say Cleopatra so Natasha had said Cleo would suffice.

"Goodbye, Tommy." She blew a kiss as she stepped out onto the street.

"Now, Natasha—" her mother began.

"I know, Mom," she interrupted. "I won't be late."

Mrs. Morris smiled as she put the car into drive and drove away from the curb.

"Have a nice time, Natasha. Goodbye."

Natasha waved at Tommy as he waved out of the back window. Then with one last pull at her wig, she joined the other students as they entered the gym.

"Over here, Natasha," she heard Olivia call. She turned to see her friend, faux cigarette holder in silken gloved hand, wearing her beaded, sequined dress and topped with a small hat with a very large feather.

"Olivia, you look terrific," she laughed as she joined her friend.

"So do you, Nat! Your makeup is fantastic! You look like a dead person reincarnated. Your eyes are so black!"

The two girls laughed together and went in search of the rest of their classmates. There was a prize for the best costume and most of the students worked hard to be in the running.

A passing gorilla growled at Olivia. Olivia laughed.

"Unfortunately, I'll never know who he is. There are at least six different gorillas here."

The girls made their way toward the end of the gym where soft drinks were being served.

"Hey, look, there's Batman over there." Natasha smiled. "And Catwoman's with him. Just look at the length of her claws, and I thought my nails were long!"

A rather silly looking cat stood beside the soft drinks table, smiling now and again at a sequined Elvis.

"Isn't this so much fun?" Natasha nudged Olivia. "Olivia, what on earth's wrong with you?"

Olivia looked like she was in some sort of trance, but the look of fear on her face told Natasha there was something very wrong. She followed Olivia's gaze to the far side of the gym to the spot they had just left and immediately saw what had caught her friend's attention. A slight, fair-haired girl had just entered the room. She wore a long, cream-colored gown that was very old-fashioned and had frills around the cuffs and hem. On the back of her head she wore a small matching bonnet.

"Oh my God!" Natasha breathed. "It can't be—can it?"

The two girls were frozen. Then Natasha felt a tug on her arm.

"Hi, girls."

Natasha turned around.

"It's me, Marcie."

Marcie was dressed in a pale blue dress with a short white apron tied around it. In her hair she wore a large headband and under her arm she had tucked a white rabbit.

Natasha tried to regain her composure. She had hoped that the girl they had been looking at in the distance was in fact Marcie, but if the girl standing beside her was Marcie dressed as Alice in

Wonderland then that ruled that possibility out!

"Hi, Marcie," Natasha said. "Olivia." She pulled on her friend's arm. "Look, isn't Marcie a perfect Alice."

Olivia turned. "Oh, yes, yes," stumbled Olivia. "Your costume's great." She tried to show some enthusiasm but kept feeling her eyes being dragged back to the slight figure at the other end of the room.

"Told you—family tradition," Marcie continued. "Apparently my great, great, great aunt, or someone, actually I'm not sure how many greats it is, knew Lewis Carroll, you know, the person who wrote Alice in Wonderland and Through the Looking Glass and based Alice's sister on her. I mean I know she only played a small part, the sister that is, but our family became very Alice-obsessed after that. Every Halloween we use it as an opportunity to indulge a little in the book's characters. I've gone as a white rabbit before, but that can get very hot and stuffy..."

Marcie's voice droned on and on in the background, and by this time Natasha wasn't paying attention.

"Marcie, I hate to be rude, but there's someone we have to talk to over there. We'll be back in a minute or two. Excuse us."

The two girls moved away and hurried to the far end of the room.

Marcie turned away, feeling slightly annoyed, and limped toward the drinks table.

As Natasha and Olivia approached, the fair-haired girl turned toward them with a smile on her lips.

"Hello, Natasha, Olivia," she murmured. "What do you think?"

Natasha and Olivia stopped in their tracks. Olivia looked quizzically at the girl. "Ellis?" she questioned.

"Darn!" said Ellis. "I knew you'd guess it was me. It's the dark eyebrows, isn't it?"

Natasha and Olivia started to breathe again. Natasha's eyes traveled to Ellis's feet, but she wore normal shoes, not a built up one like the real Suzanna.

"But who are you supposed to be?" the girls asked.

"Well, I know I'm not anyone famous," said Ellis, "but my mom found a trunk in the attic and this was one of the outfits inside. It fit perfectly, and I haven't had time to make anything because of all the time I've been spending with Scott and everything, so I decided I'd just come as a girl from the 1800s! You two look very glamorous though, maybe I made the wrong choice," finished Ellis.

"No, you look really great," Natasha managed. "We left Marcie by the drinks, so we should probably go back and get her. Are you coming?"

"Yes, in a minute or two, I just want to find Scott. He said he was dressing as a gorilla. You haven't seen him, have you?"

Olivia and Natasha rejoined Marcie.

"Marcie, I'm really sorry," said Olivia. "Let me look at your costume again."

Marcie smiled. "Well I have to admit I was a bit hurt earlier, but I'll forgive you." She twirled, showing the full flounces of the skirt with the stiff net petticoat underneath. "Don't know how they ever wore these things though," she said. "Give me a pair of sweatpants any day!"

The girls laughed. Natasha and Olivia smiled at one another.

"Come on," said Olivia, as they went on to the dance floor. "Let's have some fun!"

Just as the girls were growing tired from all the fun, the evening was coming to an end. The pumpkins had lost their glow, as had most of the guests and parents were lining their cars up outside waiting to pick up their children.

The four friends stood on the top step outside the school.

"Oh, I almost forgot," said Ellis. "My mom said I could invite you all over tomorrow since it's Saturday. Pleeeeease say you'll come. She and my dad are going out for the day and we'll have the house to ourselves. Come on, you've never been to my house before. Say you'll come."

The girls were thrilled to be invited. Ellis was right, they hadn't been to her house before.

"We'll be there," they returned.

"Great." Ellis smiled. "Come over at twelve o'clock—you too, Alice." She nudged Marcie. "And bring your white rabbit if you like!" Ellis ran off down the steps.

"Wait, Ellis, don't you want a ride?" shouted Olivia.

But Ellis was gone, ringlets streaming behind her as she ran off into the darkness.

"Oh well, seems like she didn't want a ride," Olivia said, as her father's car pulled up to the curb.

The three girls clambered in, stifling yawns as

they pulled on seat belts and yanked at annoying wigs and stiff petticoats and frowned at sequin-less patches on their dresses.

"No one turned into a pumpkin?" joked Mr. Goulden.

"No, Dad," returned Olivia, "nor did any of us meet our handsome princes."

Natasha leaned her head back against her seat and closed her eyes for the short car journey in front of her.

CHAPTER SEVEN

Gatefells

"Candy? You can't be serious, Natasha. You want to take candy with you?" Olivia couldn't believe what she was hearing from her friend.

"It's just for fun," Natasha laughed into the phone. "I mean it is the day after Halloween—maybe Ellis was planning on having us bobbing for apples—you never know. Anyway, my mom bought so much and she still has it all in the kitchen. I'll fill a few bags and bring some."

Olivia had gone quiet on the other end of the phone.

"Are you still there, Olivia?" Natasha asked.

"Yes, I'm still here, Natasha. It was just you saying

this was the day after Halloween that made me remember the date. November 1. It was on this day in 1820 that Suzanna died, remember?"

Natasha had momentarily forgotten. "Yes, I do remember, Olivia. Look, should we do what we did last night? Go to Ellis's house, have a good time, and put Suzanna in the back of our minds for now? I mean, let's face it, nothing strange has happened for a couple of days. Maybe the whole thing was in our imagination."

Olivia started to protest.

"No, okay, I know you're right, we couldn't have imagined the things that happened. Let's say that after today we look at this whole thing again, go back to the library, maybe ask Mrs. Florence some direct questions. You never know what she might be able to help us with."

Olivia took a deep breath. "Okay, Natasha, I guess you're right. I'll meet you at the bottom of the lane next to the new hospital. I'll give Marcie a call and tell her we'll wait for her there, too. See you in half an hour or so."

Olivia hung up the phone. Natasha was right. She must put this thing in the back of her mind. Suzanna Craigson was dead, and there was absolutely nothing she, Olivia Goulden, could do about that. She picked up the phone and dialed Marcie's number.

No one answered.

Strange, thought Olivia, maybe she's already gone up to Ellis's house, although I would have thought she would have wanted to meet up with Natasha and me and all go together. Maybe she went to the store to pick up some things before she goes and we'll meet her on our way.

Olivia ran upstairs to pick up her warm jacket. It was chilly outside these days, and she wasn't sure if Ellis planned for them to spend the day indoors or out. Better to be prepared.

"Hurry up, slowpoke," shouted Natasha to Olivia.

"It's freezing out here."

Olivia hurried along the pavement toward her friend.

"Sorry, I kept calling Marcie, but she wasn't answering," replied Olivia.

Natasha shrugged.

"Maybe she's already at Ellis's house—who knows? Let's hurry up, though. Hopefully she'll have something hot to drink waiting for us."

The girls began their ascent toward Gatefells. The house was situated almost at the highest point of the town, and they climbed together in silence—the silence that comes only from knowing someone your whole life.

Olivia broke the silence to ask, "Do you know what Ellis's parents do for a living, Natasha? The family certainly seems well off."

Again, Natasha shrugged. "No, I kept meaning to ask my mom, but I never did. All I know is they live in a large, fancy house on the top of this hill and that

Ellis gets everything she wants!"

The girls were now on the grounds of the old house and Natasha was struck not only by the beauty of the large yard that surrounded the house, but by the sheer size of everything.

"Wouldn't it be amazing to live here, Olivia? Look at how big everything is."

Olivia didn't answer. Since she had stepped on the grounds of the house, she had been feeling slightly on edge.

"Didn't there used to be gates here?" she asked Natasha, pointing to the edge of the lawn.

Natasha turned to look at her. "How would I know that, Olivia? I've only been by this place once or twice before, and both of those times I was in the car. As far as I know, there weren't ever any gates."

"Then how is it that I remember large wrought iron gates supported on either side by stone pillars?" asked Olivia. "And I know that that oak tree over there used to hold a swing in the summertime."

Olivia was becoming more and more animated now as she spoke. Her eyes were bright as she looked all around her.

"There, look, the window I used to sit at while Ellen prepared dinner. If you sat in a certain position just before dusk fell you could see Papa dismount..."

Natasha was staring very hard at Olivia. This whole thing had affected Olivia more than she could have imagined. Natasha took Olivia's hands in her own.

"Olivia, you have to calm down! Olivia, please!"

Olivia's eyes were wild, darting in every direction. She was smiling, laughing almost, but it was a hollow laughter which chilled Natasha's very heart.

"Olivia, please, you're scaring me. Who is Ellen? Papa dismounting? I don't know what you're talking about."

"Natasha, Olivia, over here!"

Both girls turned. Ellis was standing in the doorway of the house, waving frantically. "Come on, you two," she shouted. "I thought you'd never get here."

Natasha turned back toward Olivia, still holding both her hands. The wild-eyed look had gone, and the Olivia she knew again stood beside her.

"I'm all right, Natasha. Honestly, I don't know what happened just then. I had the strangest feeling that...oh, forget it, come on." She rubbed at her eyes as though she had just woken from a deep sleep and pulled the collar of her jacket up even more. "Ellis is waiting for us, let's go."

Both girls walked up the short path which led to the entrance of Gatefells, each of them trying to put aside their uneasy thoughts.

Ellis led them into the enormous kitchen. There was a blazing log fire in the large fireplace, and she had just made hot chocolate.

"Okay, hot chocolate with peppermint, hot chocolate with orange, hot chocolate with coconut, or hot chocolate with extra chocolate?" she offered.

"Oh, anything, just as long as it's warm." Natasha smiled. "It's really cold out there today."

Ellis turned to pour the boiling liquid into the waiting mugs and Natasha stole a glance at Olivia. She seemed to be completely back to normal. Natasha took the hot mug from Ellis gratefully and cupped both hands around it.

"Thanks, Ellis. Is Marcie here?" Natasha asked.

"Haven't seen her yet." Ellis joined the girls at the oak table. "I thought you were all coming together."

"Well, yes," said Olivia, "that was the plan, but I couldn't reach her and assumed she had come earlier on her own. Oh well, maybe we can call her again in a little bit?"

Ellis nodded. "Sure, why not. Listen, if you've started to warm up, give me your jackets and I'll hang them up for you, then we can get them when we go back outside."

"We're going outside?" asked Natasha. "My toes are just beginning to thaw out and you're talking about going back outside?"

"Oh, don't be such a wimp, Natasha." Ellis dug the girl playfully in the ribs as she walked past her to hang up the jackets. "It's only November, there's a lot colder weather to come. I thought you two would love to wander around the grounds later."

Olivia shifted in her seat.

"I, for one, would love to have a look around, Ellis. I'm very interested in the history of the place— maybe you can fill us in on the details."

Ellis smiled. "Well, my mom and dad would probably be better at that, although I do know some things. I'll try my best."

Natasha raised her eyebrows in Olivia's direction. Oh well, she thought, maybe it's for the best to find out more about this place. After all, it seems to strike a chord of recognition with Olivia, and maybe Ellis can explain some of the morning's weird events.

She helped herself to a chocolate cookie and pulled her chair closer to the open fire.

CHAPTER EIGHT

Please Don't Be a Rat

"Ellis, can I use your bathroom?" asked Olivia.

"Sure, go back out the way we came in, take your first left, then first right—you can't miss it," Ellis replied. "Meanwhile, Natasha and I will go down to the library. If you want to find out about the history of Gatefells, that's the place to do it! I'll take Natasha first, then meet you back in the kitchen."

Natasha and Ellis made their way from the kitchen down some winding stairs that led to a long narrow corridor.

"Wow!" exclaimed Natasha. "Are these your ancestors?" She looked at the rows of paintings that lined the corridor.

"Yes, some of them are," Ellis replied. "That's great uncle Nicholas and that's his wife in the small painting above his. Don't think they had any children. Okay, almost there."

The passageway was getting darker and darker the farther the girls traveled.

Suddenly, Ellis stopped in front of a door. She tried to turn the handle.

"It's a little stiff, not used very much these days."

She gave it a hefty push and the door slowly opened.

"Where's the light?" asked Natasha as she peered into the darkness. To her utter surprise and amazement she felt a push from behind.

"Ellis, what are you doing?" she almost screamed.

Ellis seemed to smile in the dark passageway and gave one final push.

"Sorry, Natasha," she muttered as she locked the door from the outside. "No hard feelings, just need to get you out of the way for now."

Natasha, plunged into blackness, had fallen down the small flight of stairs inside what appeared to be some sort of cellar.

"Ellis," she cried. "Let me out of here! If this is some sort of a game..."

She tried to stand but had hurt her ankle in the fall. Her hand felt wet when she lifted it to brush the hair from her eyes. She must have cut it on the rough edge of the stairs when she tried to break her fall.

Suddenly, something scuttled past her, and she could just about make out its shape in the darkness.

Oh God, she thought terrified and hurting, not rats, please God, not rats.

"Where's Natasha?" Olivia asked as Ellis returned to the kitchen.

"Oh, she's looking something up," she said. "Then she's joining us outside. Here, I brought your jacket."

"But aren't we going to the library with Natasha first?" asked Olivia.

"No, no," Ellis reassured her, "she said she'd only be a minute or two then she'd come and get us. Come on, let's go, and I'll show you around. I thought you were curious. Aren't you?"

Olivia took her jacket from Ellis's extended hand.

"Oh, yes, I'm curious, where should we start?"

The two girls made their way outside and around the back of the house.

"The boating lake—it's still here!" cried Olivia.

"Yes, it's still here," returned Ellis. "Why wouldn't it be?"

"Well, I just thought, you know, with Suzanna being drowned here and everything that maybe the lake would have been drained and filled in," said Olivia.

Ellis did not register surprise at the mention of Suzanna's name.

"Oh, no," replied Ellis. "These old boating lakes have their uses, you know." She smiled at Olivia.

"Let's go out in the boat! It looks old, I know, but it's completely safe."

Olivia started to follow her, then stopped in her tracks.

"Ellis, do you know the story of Suzanna? It's just that you didn't stop me just now to ask how I knew about it."

Ellis turned to face her.

"Of course I know the story. She was a relative, you know. Come on, you first. I'll hold your hand while you step into the boat."

"I'm not sure," Olivia started. "I mean, do your parents allow you..."

"Just get in, Olivia," Ellis snapped, almost pushing the girl into the boat.

"Ellis, don't push, you'll rock the boat," said Olivia, who by now was a little alarmed.

Ellis laughed.

"Don't push, Ellis, you'll rock the boat," Ellis mimicked in a childish voice. "Always the helpless little baby hiding behind Natasha. Well, Miss Goulden, I've had just about enough of your whining."

Ellis began to unfasten the boat from its moorings.

She's lost it, thought Olivia. Where on earth was Natasha? "Ellis, please stop this," she pleaded.

"Oh no," returned Ellis. "I can't stop now. I've waited years for this, don't you see? I have to avenge Suzanna. Suzanna Craigson. Remember the girl who died here? Except she shouldn't have died. Let me turn the clock back for you. Are you comfortable? Then I'll begin."

Ellis cleared her throat, while the boat started to drift slowly away from the lake's edge.

"The Craigson family—mother, father, and Suzanna, that is, settled here in the early 1800s. Suzanna was their only child, loved by both. The girl was introverted and did not make friends easily because she was self-conscious about her limp.

The townspeople frowned on newcomers in those days, especially those who were a little different. One day, however, a woman knocked on the door of Gatefells to ask whether or not the Craigsons needed a housekeeper. Mrs. Craigson was unsure at first, having managed so far to keep the house tidy on her own, but when she invited the woman in and opened the door wide, she saw the woman also had a daughter, roughly the same age as Suzanna. There was no mention of a husband, however, and Mrs. Craigson took pity on the two and hired the woman as a housekeeper, probably thinking at the same time that the young girl would be company for her own daughter.

"Ellen, the housekeeper, worked diligently from morning to night. At first, she kept her daughter with her in the kitchen, but then, finding that Suzanna would sit outside staring into the kitchen, as though she was waiting for the girl, she gradually allowed her daughter Jemma to spend time with

Suzanna. The two girls soon became inseparable and the Craigson household was filled with their laughter.

"Mr. and Mrs. Craigson were delighted with the way things were progressing and told Ellen, as she served up their evening meal, how it had been a fortunate day when she came to Gatefells. Of course, these things are never what they seem, are they?"

Ellis paused and glared at Olivia. "Just as you're probably not what you seem either, Olivia, little miss goody two-shoes. Are you scared? Wish your friend was with you?"

She laughed again and pushed the boat out a little farther with the paddle.

"Anyway, Jemma, underneath it all, really carried a big chip on her shoulder, you see. She had started off life as an illegitimate child—and it was a big deal then, you know—she felt inferior to Suzanna, and she hated having to watch her mother slave from morning to night, making sure everything was done for the Craigsons' comfort. So she came up with a plan. Very straightforward and logical, I guess, if you need to get rid of someone. Since they happen to have a boating lake right on their doorstep, she would simply need to take her out on the lake one day and drown her. She planned it right down to the smallest detail. She believed that if Suzanna was out of the picture then there was the possibility that Mr. and Mrs. Craigson would become even more attached to her, and maybe even adopt her!

"Although she didn't exactly want to be parted from her mother, being adopted would mean she would inherit the Craigsons' wealth, and she and her mother would never have to beg, borrow, or steal again. She knew Mr. and Mrs. Craigson were fond of her, and she did everything in her power to weasel her way even more into their affections.

"There used to be a boathouse here at that time, and she put dry clothes there on the fateful day in preparation for what was to come. Mr. and Mrs.

Craigson had gone into town to pick up the new dress they'd had made for Suzanna's birthday party. She would be fourteen years old the next day, and they were planning to take the girls to a fancy new restaurant that had just opened in the next town. Jemma had been given one of Suzanna's hand-me-downs to wear, a perfectly good dress which fit very well, but to Jemma, it was the final straw.

"As Mr. and Mrs. Craigson set off that morning, Jemma made sure they saw her dress in her outdoor clothes. 'I'm just going to visit old Mrs. Lawrence,' she told them. 'Mama says she's not been well recently, so I'll take over some of her herbal cough remedy to ease her chest a bit.' What a kind girl, they both thought as they waved goodbye.

"Amazing how you can just fool some people, isn't it?" said Ellis, again coming back to the present.

Olivia was as white as a sheet. Slowly, the boat was drifting steadily to the center of the lake and Olivia could feel that her feet were wet.

"Oh, didn't I tell you?" laughed Ellis. "There's a hole in the bottom of the boat. Just a small one, but big enough to let the boat fill up in about half an hour. Just long enough, I think, to make sure you're frightened half to death. Then you'll know what poor Suzanna went through!"

Olivia looked down, and sure enough, there was a hole just at the far end of the boat and a small puddle had gathered there.

"Ellis, please," she begged. "I don't understand. What does all this have to do with me? Why are you making me pay for Suzanna's death? I didn't have anything to do with it. I couldn't have, it was before I was born! Ellis, please help me!"

But Ellis just seemed to stare right through her. Her eyes now looked to be cold as steel. Olivia knew, deep in her heart, that Ellis would never help her.

"Natasha," Olivia whispered almost silently, "I need you. Please help me." A single tear started to roll down her cheek.

CHAPTER NINE

Please Hear Me

Natasha had managed to drag herself to
an upright position. Her eyes were becoming
accustomed to the dark and she could see there
was a deep cut in her hand. She took off one of her
socks, slipped her shoe back on, and wrapped the
sock around her hand as best she could. The rats she
thought she had heard earlier had either scuttled
back into the blackness or were maybe just small
mice, which were no doubt more frightened of her
than she was of them. She tried to think. She had
absolutely no idea why Ellis was doing this. All she
did know was that she had to get out of here and
fast. Who knew what sort of trouble Olivia was in?

It was beginning to get even colder in here and there were no windows, so no sunlight permeated the room. Then suddenly, Natasha saw the reason for the sudden burst of cold air. The slight figure of Suzanna Craigson had appeared in the corner of the room. Natasha limped back in fear until her back was pressed hard against the wall and she couldn't move any farther.

"Natasha, please hear me," Suzanna started. "Don't be afraid." She held out her hand toward the terrified girl. "Please, believe me! I'm here to help you. You must get out of here. Ellis has Olivia."

"Ellis has Olivia? Where?" Natasha asked. She tried to move. "Oh darn it!" She kicked at the wall in frustration, momentarily forgetting her swollen ankle and drawing back in pain.

"How can I get out of here?" Natasha asked. "There aren't any windows. The door won't budge. What am I supposed to do?"

Somewhere in the back of her rational mind, she

was thinking: I'm talking to a ghost. I've completely lost it now. I'm talking to a ghost.

For now though, rational thoughts took second place to the crisis at hand: getting out of this dark cellar and finding her friend.

Suzanna spoke again. "Natasha, you must listen to me, and listen carefully. I lived in this house once upon a time, and I know the passageways. If you follow my instructions, I can get you out of here, but you must listen very carefully."

Natasha nodded. "I'm listening."

Suzanna turned toward the wall opposite the door and pointed to a large stone that jutted out more than the others.

"If you press this, it will open a passageway that leads to the kitchen. Just inside the doorway before you proceed down the passage, put your hand into the hole in the wall on the left and you will be able to feel a candle and some matches. They have been there since my time in this house, and now you must make use of them."

Suzanna gave more directions as Natasha listened intently, trying to ignore the pain in both her hand and her ankle.

"Quickly, Natasha." Suzanna's figure started to fade. "You must hurry, there's no time to waste."

As the girl disappeared completely from view, Natasha moved toward the stone and pressed hard. As Suzanna had said, the wall began to move slowly, not having been moved for years, to reveal a large passageway. She felt to the left of her and found the candle and lit it with a match, then began to limp as fast as she could along the passageway.

The boat was almost a quarter full by now. Olivia was desperately trying not to panic as she knew any movement she made in the boat would make the situation worse. Ellis, meanwhile, had resumed her story.

"And so Jemma waited until the Craigsons were

out of sight before she went inside, discarded her outer garments, and went to seek out Suzanna. She found her outside and quickly set her plan into motion. She invited her out in the small rowing boat which was always moored to the side of the small lake and when Suzanna showed some fear, for she could not swim, Jemma quickly dispelled her doubts and reassured her that everything would be just fine. Would she, Jemma, let anything happen to her dearest friend? Suzanna smiled. She thought she was being silly. Jemma would take care of her, hadn't she always?

"The two girls went to the lake and helped one another into the small rowing boat, each holding a paddle. Jemma began to sing 'Row, row, row your boat,' and Suzanna joined in, both girls laughing together as they neared the center of the lake. Then, just at the center, the deepest part, Jemma dared Suzanna to stand up, saying that she also would stand. After some hesitation the trusting young girl did as she was told, but when Jemma stood it was to grab the girl and push her out of the boat and into the dark murky waters. Suzanna bravely tried to fight her off, her eyes wild with both fear and disbelief, but she was a small girl, and her strength could not compare to that of Jemma's. One final push and she was in the water. Jemma didn't wait to see whether or not her friend's head would bob back up, instead she rowed to the other side of the lake as quickly as she could in order to retrieve her dry clothes from the boathouse where she had placed them that morning.

"Suzanna did surface, at least twice, struggling to breathe, trying to call out for her beloved parents and fighting for her life. The last sight she saw, just before her lungs filled completely with water, was that of her friend clambering from the boat at the lake's edge, and the last emotion she felt was that of betrayal.

"Betrayal, Olivia. Is that what you're feeling? That

I've betrayed your friendship? I hope you're feeling that, Olivia. I hope you're feeling the same fear Suzanna felt, because you know that I will never help you."

Olivia, crying silently, looked at the girl standing on the shore of the lake and said nothing.

Ellis had started to speak again.

"Of course it didn't work," she continued. "The Craigsons were so distraught at the loss of their poor daughter that they couldn't even bear to look at Jemma. She reminded them of Suzanna so much.

"The final straw came one day a few weeks later when Jemma dressed up in Suzanna's new dress, the one she was going to wear to her fourteenth birthday party, thinking maybe Mr. and Mrs. Craigson would like to see her wear it and that their hearts would soften when they saw her looking so beautiful in it. Of course the silly girl only upset them even more. Mrs. Craigson was almost hysterical with grief and Mr. Craigson shut himself away in his study.

"Downstairs in the kitchen, Ellen chastised her daughter for being so vain. She was aware of her daughter's faults and that the girl could be vain, greedy, and spiteful. Although she tried to banish the thought from her mind, she wondered sometimes if Jemma had been involved in the boating accident. The Craigsons' grief was such that she felt like a complete outsider and that her daughter's presence was a constant reminder to them of Suzanna. She left some weeks later and settled in a town a few hundred miles away.

"Ellen Goulden. Does that name mean anything to you, Olivia?"

Olivia started, "Goulden. It's a common name, Ellis. Why should it mean anything to me?"

"Because you are related, that's why, Olivia. She wormed her way into poor Suzanna's heart and then disposed of her when she felt like it. Do you know what my mother's maiden name was, Olivia? Craigson. Yes, that's right, Craigson. Suzanna was family, but your greedy relative decided to snuff out her life, do away with her in order to try and inherit her money.

"Sad that it didn't work, Olivia. Us Craigsons, though, are strong. Suzanna's father had sisters and brothers scattered throughout the country and one of the younger brothers and his wife came here to Gatefells to settle down and make sure that the family line was continued. So here I am. And there you are."

Ellis glanced in Olivia's direction. Not long now, she thought. The boat was just about to topple.

"Olivia, hold on, I'm coming!"

Olivia turned in the direction of the voice. Marcie was running toward her with an older man— her father, Olivia later realized.

Ellis looked up, dismayed, only to see that Natasha, too, had escaped and was limping toward the lake. However, Marcie's father was the one who jumped into the lake and swam out toward the almost capsized boat. He was the one who pulled Olivia from the boat and half-dragged, half-swam with her back toward the bank. And he was the one who held her gently in his arms while she cried.

CHAPTER TEN

Oh, Suzanna, Thanks for Everything

The girls found out the next day that Ellis had called Marcie to tell her that the plans had been canceled and to not bother coming.

Marcie, however, returned from a shopping trip with her mother and called Natasha to meet up with her that afternoon only to be told by Mrs. Morris that Natasha and Olivia were at Gatefells! Never having trusted Ellis much anyway, Marcie suspected something was going on and asked her father to take her to Ellis's house.

That afternoon, Natasha and Olivia placed small bunches of flowers on the grave and sat quietly for a few moments before getting up to leave the cemetery.

"Goodbye, Suzanna," whispered Olivia, "and thanks for everything."

Natasha linked arms with her best friend.

"What a shame nobody could have saved her in time—guess it just wasn't meant to be," Natasha sighed. "At least we've still got you." She smiled and hugged her friend.

Natasha still limped slightly from her fall in the cellar. The doctor said it was just a very bad sprain and she should get rest as much as possible.

"No more soccer for a few weeks," she joked with Olivia.

"What do you think will happen to Ellis?" asked Olivia.

"Who knows," Natasha replied. "Probably a suspension or something. She deserves it."

Olivia turned to close the gate to the cemetery and noticed one of the graves was strewn with fresh flowers. She raised her eyes to look at the tombstone. There were only two words inscribed there: Jemma Goulden.

Read on to enjoy an excerpt from another
haunting title in the Creepers series:

The Piano

by Edgar J. Hyde

Illustrations by Chloe Tyler

CHAPTER ONE

A Stroke of Luck

Roger Houston checked his mirror, turned on his blinker, and brought the car to a stop on the side of the road. His wife, beside him, yawned and stretched.

"Where are we?" she asked sleepily.

"Somewhere named Granville. Isn't it nice?" he replied. "I think I may fall asleep at the wheel if I don't get out for awhile and stretch my legs. We better wake up the children."

The Houston family was returning from their annual Easter trip and had been driving since early that morning. Mr. Houston felt his eyes ache with the strain of driving for so long and felt the need for some refreshment.

Granville, thought Mr. Houston, looks like the perfect place to stop and have lunch.

The children, roused from sleep by their mother, were rubbing their eyes, stretching wearily, and getting ready to get out of the car.

"Don't forget your jacket, Victoria. It's colder than you think," said Mrs. Houston. "You too, Darren, where's your jacket?"

Mrs. Houston busied herself getting the children ready while her husband leaned against the outside of the car, enjoying the fresh air.

"Nice place. This really is picturesque," he said to no one in particular. "I can't believe we've never noticed it before."

His thoughts were interrupted by his family spilling noisily out onto the pavement. Darren's hair, as it typically did, stuck up in all different directions, while he could see his practically-a-teenager daughter check her reflection in the car's side mirror and smooth down her hair before making sure her metallic blue nail polish wasn't chipped.

"Dad, Mom, can we go to the toy store? Can we, please, please?" Darren bounced up and down, looking eagerly from one parent to the other as he waited for his parents to answer. Mr. Houston shook his head sternly.

"Listen, young man," he told his six-year-old son, "we have enough new toys packed in the trunk of the car without buying anymore. I'm surprised the car was able to move at all with all that weight in the back."

Darren looked momentarily crestfallen then, brightening, took his dad's hand and asked, "Can I buy some candy then, Dad, can I, please? I have five dollars left in my pocket, please."

Grabbing his son's small, sticky hand—what has that child been eating now, he thought to himself—Mr. Houston turned left onto a small side street before muttering absentmindedly, "Depends on whether or not you eat your lunch, son."

Mrs. Houston and Victoria walked behind more leisurely—Mrs. Houston admiring the pretty flower boxes adorning the fronts of the small, white houses, Victoria looking hopefully for a beauty store. As they turned onto the side street, they found Mr. Houston and Darren, noses pressed hard against a shop window. Looking up, Mrs. Houston noticed the sign above the store: Larkspur Music. She and her daughter joined the others, and they too pressed their noses against the window to see the instruments stored inside. Though everything looked pretty dusty, the family was thrilled to see a range of musical instruments: a cello, some violins, guitars, a huge drum kit that took up most of the left side of the window, and much more.

"Let's go in," Mrs. Houston said, glancing at the open sign on the front of the door. Though neither she nor her husband had any musical skills to speak of, Mrs. Houston had always wanted to be able to

play something.

Pushing open the door, the family entered the shop and there, right in the center, stood the most beautiful piano they had ever seen. Predominantly white, it stood proudly with its lid open, showing polished keys that seemed to simply cry out for someone to play them. Victoria, three years into piano lessons, was the first to run her fingers along the keys.

"Oh, Mom, Dad, it's perfect—can we buy it, please?"

Mr. Houston was aghast. "Buy it, Victoria? You can't be serious. Do you know how much these things cost? Put the lid down, you're not supposed to touch, you know."

"Don't be so hard on her, dear," Mrs. Houston intervened. "I can understand how she feels. It really is beautiful."

She too moved closer to the piano and ran her own fingers along the keys. As a child, Mrs. Houston had hoped her parents would send her to piano lessons, but unfortunately, the money was always needed elsewhere, and she had never fulfilled her dream.

"Can I help you?" came a voice from the far end of the store. An elderly man was walking toward them. "Ah, you've taken a liking to the piano, have you, my dear?" He smiled at Victoria.

"Well, yes, it is so beautiful," she said. "I didn't mean to touch it, really, I just couldn't help myself."

"Oh, don't worry about that," he returned. "Most people who come in here are drawn to the piano. Have a seat. What about you, young man? Would you like to sit on the stool alongside your sister?"

Darren was seated on the stool almost before the words had left the owner's mouth. His sister, seated half on and half off, grimaced at her brother before gently touching the keys while Darren, brasher than Victoria, began to roughly play his scales.

"Would you be interested in buying, sir, madam?"

The man smiled at them both. "I'm quite sure you'll be surprised at the price."

Mrs. Houston had no doubt about that whatsoever!

"$400," the owner was saying. "And we'll deliver it to you, free of charge."

Dad smiled. The old guy must be under the impression they want to buy the stool!

"Now what on earth would be the point in having a stool with no piano?"

"$400?" Mrs. Houston turned quizzically to the man. "Does that include the stool?"

Though disbelieving of the price, she wasn't one to waste an opportunity!

"Yes, of course, madam. The piano, the stool, and delivery. We can get it to you by, say, Monday morning." Checking the wall calendar quickly, he nodded in confirmation. "Yes, Monday should be fine. Now, if you'd just give me your address, we'll fill out the form. Tedious, all the forms you have to complete these days."

And just like that, the piano belonged to the Houston family. Dad left the shop in a complete daze, having filled in and signed a check for $400, given his name, address, and phone number to the owner, and stuffed a receipt in his wallet.

"Oh, don't look like that, Roger," said Mrs. Houston. "It's such a stroke of luck, finding an instrument in that condition, and at that price."

Taking both her children by the hand, she strode off in front of her husband, leaving him to shake his head over the events that had just taken place.

CHAPTER TWO

Strange Music

"Here comes the truck now!" shouted Darren from upstairs.

He had been keeping watch since eight that morning, excited about the delivery of the piano, and now could hardly contain himself. Throwing himself down the stairs, he was the first to the front door, almost tripping over a stray skate.

The truck pulled up outside the house and two men got out, made their way to the back of the truck, and unlocked the doors. Mr. Houston by now had appeared outside, and he directed the men to put the piano into the large room that was used partially for storage and partially for the children's toys. Everything in the room had been frantically pushed to one side that morning in order to make room for the family's new prized possession. Mr. Houston paid the men a little something extra, thanked them graciously, and shut the door, shaking his head disbelievingly; he had truly never believed the family would ever see the piano again.

"Let me sit down! Let me sit down!" shouted Darren, as both children tried to push themselves onto the piano stool.

"It's not big enough for both of us," his older sister replied. "Get off—it's my turn first—you can't even play piano."

"Now, now," Mrs. Houston intervened, "no fighting. What we'll do is have one hour for Victoria followed by one hour for Darren. Victoria first. Darren, come over here beside me and let your sister play."

Turning to her daughter, she continued, "And since you know so much more about the piano than

Darren does, why don't you try and help him? Let's be constructive instead of arguing with one another."

Victoria shrugged and turned her full attention to the gleaming keys, while Darren stared at the clock, willing the next hour to pass quickly.

And so the day passed, with both parents being aware of scales being practiced, hearing the odd notes of "Chopsticks," intermingled with the children having the occasional argument. At the end of the night, everyone climbed wearily into bed and fell fast asleep.

𝄞   𝄞   𝄞

Mr. Houston was the first one to wake up the next morning. He looked at his alarm clock—7:30 a.m.! He nudged his wife.

"Emily? Do you hear that?"

Reluctantly she turned to face him. "What is it dear? I'm sleepy."

Then, realizing her husband was sitting up in bed, she rubbed her eyes and sat up too. It was only then that she became aware of the strange and beautiful music drifting upstairs.

"Listen," said her husband. "Can you hear it now? Come on, let's go downstairs. I didn't realize Victoria was so accomplished."

The parents both made their way to the top of the stairs and began their descent. The music still played, a haunting melody, which neither of them seemed to have heard before. They went down the stairs quietly, not wanting to disturb Victoria, and somehow unwilling to cut into the perfection of the music.

As they reached the last stair and rounded the hallway leading to the room that housed the piano, Mr. Houston stopped and gasped. He could see, in the far corner of the room, Victoria shuddering!

"Victoria! What's going on? It can't possibly be Darren playing, can it?"

As both parents ran into the room, they were aware of their small son joining them from behind.

"Why is everybody up so early?" he was

mumbling. "What's going on?"

His parents and sister did not answer, and as he followed their gaze, he realized why. The piano was playing itself!

Victoria seemed very frightened, she being the one who had first heard the music and the first one downstairs. Mrs. Houston reached out to pull her close. She was also very shaken by what she saw, and as the whole family looked on, the piano continued to play, changing tempo, getting faster and faster, louder and louder, making a great thumping sound which threatened to wake the whole neighborhood. The beautiful strains of music they had heard from upstairs now seemed angry and frenzied, and the family could do nothing but wait until the piano eventually fell silent.

The family too was silent, shocked, and stunned by what they had all just witnessed. Victoria was visibly shaking and her mother had turned a ghastly shade of white. Mr. Houston was the first to speak.

"Well, what on earth was all that about?" he said, sitting down on the nearest chair and pulling Darren onto his knee.

"Oh no, I didn't want it to stop!" said Darren. "That was fun!"

"Fun?" echoed Victoria. "Don't be ridiculous. It was terrifying! How did it play its own keys? No one was touching it. It's not one of those windup ones, is it, Mom? You know, the kind you turn the key and the piano plays certain songs?" She looked at her mom hopefully.

"I don't think so," replied Mrs. Houston, and even though before she had been pretty sure this wasn't the case, she decided to go and look. She and Victoria checked everywhere they could think of—underneath, on top, behind, even the pedals for any clues as to what might have just happened.

"Nothing there, I'm afraid," said Mrs. Houston, finally giving up.

The family sat around in silence, each with their

own thoughts.

No wonder it was such a bargain, Mr. Houston was thinking to himself. It must be haunted or something. Just as the thought entered his head, he dismissed it, reminding himself he didn't believe in ghosts!

The ringing of the doorbell shook them again. Darren jumped up from his dad's knee and ran toward the front door to see who it was. It was Simon from two doors down.

"Hey, Darren, didn't know if you were back or not. Are you going back to school today?"

Mr. Houston looked at his watch. Ten minutes until 8 a.m.! What on earth was Simon doing at the front door over an hour before school!

Victoria reluctantly got to her feet.

"I guess I better start getting ready for school, too. What a weird start to the day," she yawned as she started to climb the stairs.

Mr. and Mrs. Houston looked at each other.

"Well, do you have any explanation?" Mrs. Houston asked.

Mr. Houston looked thoughtfully at the piano. "Trick of the light? We imagined the whole thing? Who on earth knows? Let's go get some breakfast. I think better on a full stomach."

The Piano
ISBN: 9781486718764

Cold Kisser
ISBN: 9781486718740

The Gravedigger
ISBN: 9781486718795

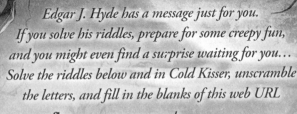

Edgar J. Hyde has a message just for you.
If you solve his riddles, prepare for some creepy fun,
and you might even find a surprise waiting for you…
Solve the riddles below and in *Cold Kisser*, unscramble
the letters, and fill in the blanks of this web URL

www.flowerpotpress.com/__ __ __ __ __ __

with the answers you find. Go to the website
with your parent's permission and find out
what waits on the other side.

1. Research can be an important part of solving a mystery, especially when that mystery involves the paranormal. Natasha and Olivia decided to look through newspapers to find evidence of Suzanna Craigson's life. What was the first letter of the location they went to in their school to find this information?

2. In this group of girls, one was not who she seemed to be. A conniving trickster, she was the one who tried to leave Olivia alone in a sinking boat in the middle of a lake. What letter does her first name start with?

3. According to Olivia, a costume for the school's Halloween dance is not complete without a bit of accessorizing. To fully complete Natasha's costume, Olivia gives Natasha a snake made from a leather belt. She refers to the snake as a specific one from Egypt. What letter does this term end with? Hint: It's also the fifth letter of who Natasha dressed up as.